In the Mirror

Abby Woodland

Published by Abby Woodland, 2024.

This is a work of fiction. Similarities to real people, places, or events are entirely coincidental.

IN THE MIRROR

First edition. February 13, 2024.

ISBN: 979-8223787983

Written by Abby Woodland.

Also by Abby Woodland

The Raze
The Dragon Keeper
Birchwood
The Fairwing School for Troubled Girls
While She Sleeps
Secrets in the Woods
In the Mirror

Watch for more at www.abbywoodland.com.

Table of Contents

Look inside and decide who you want to be, then be it.

Chapter 1

"When you look in the mirror, what do you see?" Dr. Adam Swanson was sitting in an oversized chair, looking at a thin man with greasy brown hair. His patient, James Enderson, had been coming to his office every week for the past three years and was now staring into a mirror in Adam's office. James's family had requested Dr. Swanson's help, as James had been telling everyone that there were evil people in his mirror.

"I told you before, doc, it's the same as always. My reflection changes, then speaks to me. He asks me for my help in getting free. He wants to come out of the mirror and take my place. He says there's a man trying to kill me. He says I'd be safer in the mirror. Though, I don't see him now."

"Do any other people hear their reflections?" Adam asked his patient.

"No, just me at the moment. He says that the man trying to kill me doesn't want reflections to be noticed. Not until it's time to come out. That day will be soon, doc. Soon, they will all start moving and changing and talking. Soon, when people touch their mirrors, the reflections will touch them back. Then they will switch places and people will be stuck. They won't be able to switch until their reflections touch the mirrors. But I know they plan to break the mirrors and trap us all there forever. So, don't touch the mirrors."

Dr. Swanson sat in silence for a minute, contemplating this. He wasn't sure what to think. In school, paranoid schizophrenic behavior warranted a lot of medication and overnight hospital stays. However, his story stayed the same for three years and only gets more detailed as it went on. That was something very uncommon. Either his patient was literally living this hallucination and was sicker than he seemed, or he was being one hundred percent truthful, which seemed absolutely ridiculous. But then again, this was his only hallucination and those with schizophrenia usually had several or changing visions.

Dr. Swanson wrote everything James said on his clipboard. Clearly, this was a case that would need to be brought home again, as he had so many times before, since his patient never wavered from his story and, technically, seemed to get worse. Making a note to have this patient possibly institutionalized in a long-term facility after all these years, he rose from his chair.

"Thank you so much for coming to your session, James. I hope you found it helpful." He said this to all of his patients at the close of each session. This helped him get feedback. Some would always say that it helped, but not James. Not today.

"Please, Dr. Swanson. I know what you guys think of me. I know I sound crazy. A few years back, I'd have agreed. But I'm not. It's time for them to come out into our world. I can't stop them. I've been telling everyone to stop touching mirrors and to cover them up. I've lost all the people I care about because of this. But I wouldn't say it if it wasn't true. I promise I'm not schizophrenic. If I had been, wouldn't my family have noticed my issues sooner? It's time for the mirror people to take over. They are more powerful in our world. They are the connections between the living and the dead. All the old stories are true. You can trap spirits in the mirrors, but you can trap people too. I can't save everyone by myself."

"I understand, James. Thank you for sharing. I will take that into consideration. Have a wonderful evening. Don't forget to reschedule with Maggie on your way out."

James left looking a bit more haggard and sadder than usual. He always looked tired and stressed, though, so Dr. Swanson brushed it off and started collecting his files to bring home. How did people view the mirror as such an evil thing? In his option, it was just glass. Nothing harmful about that unless you broke it. Putting a box of files and notes in the back of his car, Dr. Swanson saw his reflection in the car window, and jumped. It's nothing to be afraid of. It's just a reflection.

Stop being dumb, Adam. You're a psychologist, for goodness sake. Pull it together. This is NOT rational thinking. He thought to himself. He opened the driver's side door and climbed in, driving the road he had taken a thousand times between work and home. And there was nothing unusual about that.

Chapter 2

Adam walked in the front door and into his home office. He set down all the files he was carrying on top of his large, oak desk and took a deep breath. While he hated bringing his work home, he felt that this time it was necessary to help James out and sort this particular part of his psychosis, *if* that's what it was. There had to be a way to help him get better. It's just going to be a challenge. There was a small knock on the door.

"Hey sweetie. Can I come in?" Julia's voice floated in, and Adam instantly felt more relaxed.

"Of course." He stood up and walked over to her, wrapping his arms around her, and kissing her softly.

"How was your day?" Julia asked.

"Stressful. I had to bring some stuff home today. But I'd love to take a break for now. Should we eat dinner and watch a movie?" Adam and Julia had rules of spending at least 2 hours together each day, no matter how crazy life got to be. It worked well for them, and both partners always felt closer when they did.

"I'd love that. Lucky for you, I made fettuccini alfredo for dinner. Your favorite." She kissed him on the cheek.

"Thank you, my love." He smiled at her. She was always so sweet to him. She looked extra beautiful tonight too.

They went to the dining room that was beautifully laid out with their wedding china. They enjoyed using it as often as possible to make each day feel special. His mom always told him that you should use the pretty dishes, wear the nice suit, and listen to your favorite song because you never know when you won't get another chance.

Julia served out the meal and James briefly left Adam's mind. They made small talk as most couples do, talking about their days, chatting about household projects, and the like. If Adam could stay in this moment with her forever, he would. He really enjoyed being able to relax with his wife and not worry about mirrors or people crying all the time.

"I have an announcement to make before we watch the movie." Julia said, as she was clearing up the dishes.

"Ok, what is it?" Adam asked. He started putting away the leftovers as she walked to the sink.

"Today, I went to the doctor's office and found out that we are expecting!" She walked over to her purse that was on the kitchen counter and pulled out a sonogram of their baby. It looked like a bean, but it was their bean and Adam couldn't be more excited. He ran over to her, scooping her up and kissing her.

"That's amazing! I'm so excited! I can't wait!" He told her, constantly kissing her face and then her stomach. "We get to be parents!" He couldn't help but do a little dance, making his wife laugh. "We should go to the store and start getting things ready for the baby!" He searched for his keys, but Julia grabbed his hands.

"I am only 9 weeks along, so there's plenty of time to get ready. But I thought I'd tell you first so we can let our families know together." She told him gently, still smiling at his excitement.

"I can't wait to let them know. I should really finish painting our spare room right now! That'd be perfect for a nursery since it's close to our room." Adam replied. Julia started laughing again.

"Absolutely. I was online looking at cribs and things today but again, we still have time so let's not rush anything just yet." She told him. Adam started to calm himself down. He couldn't resist being happy about it.

"Sounds good, my love." Adam said. He hugged and kissed his wife again. They finished cleaning up and changed into their pajamas. Adam and Julia cuddled up on the couch and watched their favorite movie. Some sort of feel good comedy. Then Julia went up to bed and Adam headed to his office, ready to work for an hour or two.

He opened the first file; this was about James. He scanned through it, not knowing what he was looking for, but he already knew everything about James. He didn't really need the file at all to be honest. He closed that one and opened another one. This one was on an elderly patient with schizophrenia. She wasn't his patient, but she did belong to one of the other patients in his office. He had borrowed it to help him research more about schizophrenia and see if he could get more insight for the issues James was having.

Reading through her file, he noticed she'd been a long-term patient too. She'd been in and out of offices for several years. Digging in deeper, he noticed that when she started therapy she was saying things that were similar to what James was saying. She watched her reflection move at random in the mirror, heard voices coming from every mirror she passed, and even claimed that some of her friends and family members had been replaced by mirror versions of themselves.

He pulled out James' file again. Many things lined up exactly even though Mary Ellen McClure was a patient fifty years ago and was now only being seen for depression brought on by her Alzheimer's disease. Now at 83, she has no memory of this. James, being 27, however, has a full memory of what he's saying. It's just too uncanny they'd say the same things about the same event for it to not be true. He wondered if there were other patients experiencing the same thing.

Chapter 3

A dam decided that two patients having similar issues were more than enough to dig into everything. He luckily had access to several offices, having worked psychiatric for both inpatient and outpatient clinics. He wasn't sure how far to look back, but he decided that he'd keep following the trail backwards from this year, until it ran dry.

Adam got in his car and drove up to the Roxburgh Asylum. They had the oldest files in the county. If he was going to find a clinical pattern in patient psychosis, that would be the place to look. He parked in the visitors' spot and headed in. At reception, he saw one of his mentors, Dr. Basu. He was older than dirt but still very energetic and always the first to help a patient or, in Adam's case, a new resident. As Adam approached him, Dr. Basu looked up and smiled at him, walking around the desk to greet his former student.

"Dr. Swanson! Wonderful to see you again. How's your family?" Dr. Basu shook Adam's hand with both of his.

"My wife is doing wonderful. We just found out she's expecting!" Adam told him and his Dr. Basu's smile grew bigger.

"Such great news. Children are a wonderful blessing. You will both be such wonderful parents. So, what brings you back to our neck of the woods?" He asked, curiously.

"I have a bit of a complex patient case. Most likely borderline schizophrenia, but could also have some delirium and psychosis, too. I'm not sure though. He has similarities with another patient being seen at my office and it's so specific of a hallucination that I am questioning if it isn't real. So, I'm trying to get some research done. Haven't found much yet, but I'm hopeful something might emerge." Adam confided in him. Dr. Basu listened to all of this intently before shaking his head.

"Sounds like you have a great plan. Then I will leave you to your discoveries. Don't let your patients get to you with their ramblings, Adam. And feel free to reach out if I can be of any help and definitely call me later too. Padma and I would be happy to have you and Julia over for dinner." He advised him.

"Sounds like a great idea. Thank you, Karan." Adam grabbed his visitor's badge from the nurse at the desk and followed the wall signs down to the patient record archives. He knew Dr. Basu was right. He always gave the best advice to him when he needed it most and he shouldn't let anything James says get inside his head. He thought about turning around and going back home, but something nudged Adam forward and he kept moving.

While going downstairs, Adam's leg started to cramp. He was out of shape, and it was obvious. He was far too busy working all the time and rarely had time to work out. This made him question why all the records from former patients were kept in the basement or downstairs storage room of some sort. It was logical, of course, especially for records you didn't need access to often, and to help preserve patient privacy laws as most people won't have an access point for the basement. But Adam always found basements to be creepy, cold, and unnerving. He took three deep breaths and grounded himself. Looking around, he noted that he was just fine and most of his overthinking was based on the nature of his research rather than facts about his situation. Creepy cases equal creepy vibes and he knew that. This case was no exception to the rules.

Adam opened the steel door at the bottom of the stairs using the key he picked up at reception. The basement here wasn't so bad. There was carpet in the archive room, making it not as cold as the tile floors everywhere else, even though all asylums were kept cold to reduce germ spread in close quarters. There were a few wooden tables and chairs stacked in the corner to the left, and one table and four chairs set up in a space to the right. The rest of the room was full of dusty shelves stacked high with files, and along the back wall, there were boxes with even more files. There was a lot to go through since this asylum had been around for more than a century.

An old Macintosh desktop computer was by the first row of shelves for anyone looking for files. Clearly no one has updated the system since 1998. He avoided the headache of wrestling with dial-up and floppy disks and moved directly to the file boxes at the back wall. This would most likely be where he could find the files he needed.

The boxes were full of both new and old files mixed in. Someone hadn't kept them separated. At least they labeled most of the boxes with dates for what was inside. Adam lifted the dusty lid of the first box and started pulling out files, one by one, only leaving out the ones that talked of mirror people. It was rare, he could admit that. Not many people had mentioned that in most cases of schizophrenia. This was both nerve wracking and reassuring at the same time. Maybe the other files were just a coincidence?

Three hours of searching and he had found little outside of the ordinary claims that most mental health patients have and only one or two files that talked about their reflections staring at them, which he kept out. By the 9th box, Adam felt a bit discouraged. He was hoping for a larger number of cases to validate his patients' claims. He didn't have much luck up until now. Until this box. He found several files backing James's claims. It was labeled from 1888 to 1932 and almost every file contained something about mirror people.

Adam's heart raced, and he started frantically searching patient by patient. Some patients reported their family members as being stolen by something or someone after coming in contact with a mirror and being replaced by mirror people who weren't their loved ones. Some even reported hearing voices in the mirrors themselves. And many more even claimed that their reflections were moving without them. Most of the doctors blamed the spiritualism boom during that time with Houdini and other magical shows growing in popularity, as a way of making these people scared and confused. A lot of these people were hoping to see ghosts or visions of the dead, as most people that time would. Thus, making more sense to Adam as he read on. But what about James? He didn't live during that time. Why would he be captivated by the mumblings of people who lived long before him?

One thing Adam had noted was that many of the people reporting these things also saw a spiritualism act that was performed by a man named Samuel Gray who studied under another well-known spiritualist Harry Houdini. Gray wanted to be

Houdini's assistant but was not adept with the acts and often fumbled them or messed them up somehow. Houdini had to let Gray go, but he would go on to practice and start performing on his own a in 1921. Adam signed this box of files out and stopped in at the library to see what he could find on Samuel Gray, if he could find anything at all.

Chapter 4

At the library, Adam hoped Samuel Gray would be easier to find than he was. Unfortunately, he wasn't. He had been at the library since 2:00 in the afternoon and was there till their 9 p.m. closing time. He had only found 6 articles about Samuel Gray. The first was that he was Houdini's new assistant, the second about some large argument they had on stage, the third was about their split, the fourth about his new solo act, the fifth about his first show, and the sixth about his disappearance without a trace.

The first three were not as interesting, as Adam already knew that background, though he kept them out just in case he needed them. The rest of the articles, however, were very interesting. His show was based on using mirrors to conjure spirits and trap and transport their souls to another dimension. Furthermore, it mentioned that something horrible happened in his show to several people, and now, he was scared. Many people claimed he opened some type of portal, allowing spirits and demons to enter our world through the mirrors rather than creating a sort of travel for the living. That he caught the attention of a completely different world and that the spirits from the other side took him. Or so the article said. That could be why the police listed him as vanished. No one would believe a crowd of people who claimed to see a man get sucked into a mirror, no matter how many eyewitnesses there were.

Adam didn't really believe in this type of stuff either. He thought that maybe Samuel Gray was just a good illusionist and tricked far too many people. But there was one article he found that he hadn't been looking for. A medical journal had placed an article in the newspaper claiming schizophrenia cases were growing in numbers shortly after the performance by one... Samuel Gray. Many people are claiming to have conversations with their mirror selves. Friends and family were worried. It was almost like an epidemic.

He read on to see that even though there were over 3,000 cases, but only 60 of them seemed to have been properly documented. They sent most of those people to asylums and they never got out. And to make things worse, they all claimed to be part of James's theory about mirror people replacing real people.

Adam leaned back in the plastic chair and ran his hands through his hair. This was insane! But logically, how could so many people who were born so far apart be wrong about the same thing? There really was no explanation for this, was there? And if James was right, that meant that mirror people would replace real people soon. How could this be possible?

Adam left the library, got in his car, and headed home. Thinking of his wife and baby, he wasn't sure how to keep them safe. The baby especially, as he did not know how to keep a small child away from mirrors, especially as they got older. He also wondered what would happen if you got trapped. How would you get back out? From what he understood of mirror traps, two mirrors had to line up perfectly and stay that way so the soul couldn't escape their reflective eternity. Adam made a mental note to research how to form a mirror trap when he got home.

As he pulled into the driveway, something felt off. Julia was sitting on the porch waiting for him. She normally didn't do that. She stood up when she saw him.

"Adam, where have you been? I've tried calling you all day!" She was always worried about him.

"Sorry, I had to do some research for a client. Is everything ok?"

Julia hesitated before taking a deep breath, then said, "Yeah, everything is fine. Just felt a bit crowded in the house. Needed some air. Must be the baby."

"Alright, you let me know if there's anything more to it though, ok?" He kissed her gently on the lips. Still, something felt off. Adam just didn't know what.

They both walked inside the house with a heavy feeling hanging over them, Julia using her left hand to open the door instead of her right.

Chapter 5

A dam had been going through the motions since looking up Samuel Gray. He had very little time to research any further than he had as most of his clients needed to change their schedules thanks to the upcoming holidays. By the time November came around, he'd spent more time in the office dealing with patients worried about family feuds at dinner than he was on James and his issue. He had almost forgotten about James and the mirror people completely, but when James started missing his appointments, Adam became worried.

James had been coming in for weekly visits, but around November 1st, he'd stopped coming all together. Adam reached out and tried to get back in touch, but every message he left went unanswered. He dropped it for now but couldn't help wondering if he was ok. At lunchtime on November 22nd, Adam decided he needed some air. He told his office staff he was heading out to the I across the street. It was a perfect fall day with leaves of all different colors, floating in the air that was fresh with rain. Adam walked into the café down the street and got a large hot chocolate, broccoli and cheddar soup, and a cinnamon roll, then sat at a table by the window.

Taking a few bites, he noticed a few tables over that James was sitting there, his drink and pecan roll looked untouched. He was staring at Adam intently, but his hands seemed nervous. As a therapist, Adam clearly couldn't go up and talk to his patient in public. But he felt as though there was something wrong with him. Adam finished up his lunch, deposited his trash in the receptacle, and headed for the door with the intent of leaving another message for James on his phone back in the office. He was just about to cross the street when James caught up with him.

"Hey doc, can we set up a meeting soon?" He asked, fidgety, looking around.

"Sure. I have about an hour before my next appointment, so I can get you in now. Would that be ok?"

"Yes. Thanks." James followed Adam. They walked across the street and went up to Adam's office. He motioned for James to have a seat in the usual spot.

"What's on your mind, James?" Adam asked.

"A mirror person almost took me the other day." James whispered.

"Really? Can you tell me what happened?" Adam was more interested in the conversation now. A few of the people he researched had stated this too.

"I was brushing my teeth and trying not to look at the mirror. I have all of them covered, but the one in the bathroom, I must have bumped it because the towel I had on there fell off. The next thing I know, I feel these cold, stiff, corpse like hands wrap around my neck. I struggled and got them off of me, but the mirror broke. I barely got away. Also," he dropped his voice as low as he could, so Adam had to lean in closer, "the whispering is getting louder. I think it's time. I think they want to come over soon."

"I see. That sounds scary. No wonder you look nervous." This made Adam feel nervous too.

"That's not the half of it. If they are coming for me, they are probably coming for everyone else, too. Have you seen them anywhere or heard them?" Adam thought about Julia for a moment. She had been acting stranger than normal. But that could be pregnancy hormones. He shrugged it off.

"Not really. Though I will keep my eyes opened for them."
Adam reassured him.

"Please do. Be very careful. And if someone gets taken, don't
break their mirror. That makes it harder for them to come
home." And with that, James got up and left.

All day, Adam thought about what James said. Maybe, on
the slight chance that he's right, it was time to not have so many
mirrors in the house. He knew his wife loved having mirrors to
decorate with as she said the house felt larger that way, and there
were at least 5 in the house not counting the bathrooms. Maybe
he could convince her to replace them with some art for the time
being. His day ended, and he got in his car and went home.

When Adam pulled up in the driveway, the front door was
opened. Julia. He jumped out of the car and rushed to the front
door, pulling out his phone. Slowly stepping inside, Adam noticed there were shards of glass all over the wooden floors. Someone must have broken in. He had to find his wife now.

"Julia?" He called out. No answer. "Jules? Honey, are you
home?" He stepped gingerly around inside, hearing the crunch
of glass under his cheap Target dress shoes as he went. He saw
the main floor was clear, so he headed upstairs to the bedroom,
afraid of what he might find. Julia was lying on the bed, staring
up at the ceiling, completely still. It seemed as if she was asleep
with her eyes open.

"Julia? Are you ok?" He didn't see any blood, which was
good. Julia slowly sat up in bed, reminding him of Dracula rising
from his coffin.

"Yes, dear, I am fine." Her voice sounded awkward. Adam
was feeling nervous, though he couldn't pin point why.

"What happened to the mirrors?" Adam asked her, noticing they were all smashed on the ground. This was a bad sign.

" They are broken." She replied, giving him a wide, toothy grin.

" I see that. Any particular reason?" Though Adam knew the answer already.

"I smashed them." She started laughing and Adam felt scared and sick. His life just became a horror movie now.

"Why did you smash them?" Adam could feel a lump in his throat and wondered if it would be unprofessional to call James right now.

" So, she can't come through." He knew it. Juila had disappeared and was now replaced by her reflection. All he could do was nod his head as he turned and walked away, trying not to let her know he knew what was going on. He needed to be somewhere safe. Adam went down to his office and locked the door.

Chapter 6

A dam wasn't sure how long Julia had been gone, but he did know that it had been a few days since she sat on the front porch and waited for him. Did the taking happen gradually? The thought of living with her mirror twin was terrifying, though. He'd have to act normally and not raise suspicion. He'd also realized he'd have to talk to James again and figure this out. Only James knew how to get her back. He'd have to talk to him.

Even though he was meeting with clients as usual, Adam's distraction was evident. He was eagerly awaiting his appointment later that afternoon with James and was scared to talk to him about what he had found. He'd also considered talking to some of the other patients whom he'd researched at the library and even trying to find some descendants of Houdini and Samuel Gray. Adam hoped that someone, somewhere would know what happened to Julia and what Gray did to open the portal in the mirrors.

When twelve o'clock rolled around, Adam was expecting James to walk in. But he never showed. This added even more worry to Adam's already racing thoughts. If James wasn't here, where was he? Had the mirror people gotten him too? Since it was now lunchtime, Adam grabbed his coat and looked up at James' address. If he wasn't in the office, he was bound to be at home.

Adam pulled up to a small white house with a fairly clean yard and a white fence with a small gate around it. It was not the type of place he'd thought a haggard, mentally I'll man would live in. Then he reminded himself James wasn't as crazy as he sounded. He parked at the edge of the street and approached the front door, hearing the gate creak shut behind him. As he knocked, he realized the door was slightly ajar.

"Hello? James? Are you in here? It's Adam!" He pushed the door open slightly. Where was James? "Hello!" He cried out again. No answer. Adam pushed the door open and stepped inside. He wasn't sure what he'd find. A bunch of broken mirrors? A new James? Or just a patient having a breakdown? He was hoping it was the latter, since that was easier to deal with than this.

"James? Where are you? Is anyone here?" Adam was growing more nervous by the second. As he walked further into the home, he noticed different colored sheets covering all the mirrors. So, this is what James was talking about when he'd said to cover the mirrors. Smart. Adam thought of all the smashed mirrors at his house and wished he'd done it before the mirror Julia got the real one.

Every downstairs room Adam had entered was clear of any signs of James or mirror James, so he went up the stairs and checked the top floor. As he passed the bathroom, Adam saw where James had fought off the mirror people. There was plenty of stuff on the floor that he hadn't bothered to clean up. It was off-putting compared to the rest of the tidy home. Shampoo bottled, the soap dish, and toothbrushes were littering the floor and the mirror looked as if someone had smashed it with their fist. Adam avoided going in there since there was still glass on the floor.

Adam approached the bedroom and knocked on the closed door. There was no sound coming from inside, so he opened the door and found James lying on the ground gasping for air with a shard of glass sticking out of the side of his neck. Luckily there wasn't much blood, meaning that a main vein or an artery either hadn't been hit or was being stopped by what Adam now saw was a piece of mirror in his neck.

"James! What happened?" Adam rushed over and grabbed the blanket off the end of the bed. He used it to stabilize the mirror shard and James' neck to prevent further injury.

"Your wife." He gasped. "She was here. Took my journal. Can't stop them without it." His breathing became more labored, and Adam knew there wasn't much time to save him. Adam pulled out his phone and called for an ambulance but shortly after giving them the address, his phone died.

"Ok. They should be here soon. I'm guessing there're instructions on how to save everyone, right? In your journal?" James nodded. "So, I just need to get it back and all I need to know is there, right?" Adam asked him.

"Yes." James said, barely audible.

"Ok. I will get that back, but right now, we need to wait for the ambulance. They have the address, they should be here soon. Keep your eyes open and stay with me, James." The paramedics took about ten minutes to show up and they rushed inside the home since the door was already opened. Adam called for them to meet him upstairs and they whisked him off to the hospital for surgery while Adam was left to wonder what to do next.

Chapter 7

A dam checked in on James every day since the incident. He was relieved to find out that James's jugular wasn't hit. But after throat surgery, James still wasn't able to talk and depended on paper and pen or a communication card that the hospital had provided to converse. This made talking to him very limited as they couldn't speak about what had really happened. He also had police outside his hospital room door as medical staff saw this was an attack. Thankfully, James said he didn't know his attacker for the time being. This bought them both time.

On the day they released James, he could talk softly and needed to see a speech therapist and occupational therapist in order to get his neck working and his voice back to par. Adam came and picked him up, as he had no one else to help him right now. And he wasn't about to ask family from out of state to come stay with him after being stabbed by a mirror version of his therapist's wife.

"Don't let anyone know I'm doing this," Adam said to James. "Therapists aren't supposed to be this involved."

James whispered, "That's ok. I understand. I'm pretty sure that under these circumstances, anything goes." He tried to laugh but got fought in a coughing fit. Adam patted his back and helped him readjust the gauze over his stitches. If anything, James needed rest. They could talk about things later.

Adam helped James into the front seat of the car, tossing his clear plastic bag of belongings into the back seat. It was amazing how an entire person's life could be contained in such a small bag. Wallet with family photos, keys to a home, money from their job, it was all so insignificant now. At least James was alive.

Adam wanted to ask James more questions, but he was exhausted and to be fair, Adam wasn't looking forward to hearing how the mirror version of his wife tried to kill his client, or how she even got his address in the first place. He just left him alone, riding to his house in silence, hoping for the chance to get some much needed information. When they pulled to James' home, Adam helped James get in and settled before deciding to ask about the book.

"James, try not to strain your voice, ok? I just need to ask you about your book. I need to know what was in it." Adam said as he tucked him into his bed. There was still blood and glass on the floor and Adam made a reminder to clean it up before he left.

James adjusted himself on his pillows before speaking. "The book contained the notes I've been gathering from my mirror self. Apparently, mirror me is a bit of a rebel. He says he doesn't care about coming out into the world. He thinks that where he's at is just fine. I wasn't sure I could trust him at first, but everything he's told me has been helpful so far. He has given me information on mirrors and the world they live in. To be honest, I don't know if he's being honest or not. But he may want out eventually, so I don't know if this is a trick or if it's real." James coughed and got a drink of water before continuing.

"The book I've been keeping has all the information I've gotten from him. I've been keeping track. I think mirror me is communicating with your mirror wife, though. How else could she have known that I had the book and all that information? I think he got me to trust him by giving me real information, then trying to kill me so no one would know or have access to the information he gave me. I know if I'm dead, mirror me can come out without trapping me there first. No one would even know the difference. My soul would be trapped there though, and I'd be stuck there even if mirror me went back in. Since I didn't die, I'm sure they aren't happy about their plan."

This was too much for Adam. "I have to get that book back from her. I have to find a way to get the information in it. We need it to get the portal closed and make these things stop." Adam was furious. It was bad enough his wife was taken and his unborn child, but who knew what was going to happen now. Especially since they knew that the mirror people were out for blood too.

"I know. I have memorized some things, but not enough to stop them. I know they have their own plans, but I don't know how to find out what those are. We need to stay as far ahead of their plans as possible." Jame told him.

"We need someone. Like an illusionist. One that's able to close the portal that Gray opened after they fired him from Houdini's show." Adam said. Maybe someone like that could help them figure this out and close the portal. Surely, they would know how. It can't be that complicated now, can it?

"Actually, it needs to be the descendant of Gray. He opened the portal. Only his line of illusionists can close it. We need to find his family." James said. Adam agreed.

"I think I know a friend who can help us look for one. I have to ask him and see what he says about it. Will you be ok here while I pay him a visit?" Adam was nervous to leave James behind, but he had no choice. James needed to rest and stay as far away from danger as possible, and Adam needed to close the portal.

"Sure. But before you leave, could you hand me that?" James pointed to a fireplace poker sitting in the corner of his bedroom next to a small fireplace. How did Adam miss that even being there? He handed him the poker and James buried it next to him in bed, the sharp end he put under his pillow. "Thanks. Now I have a way to fight back... if I need it." He told him. Adam hoped that James wouldn't need it though.

"Get some rest and call if you need me." Adam told him. Then he left.

Chapter 8

Adam headed over to the city census bureau. His friend Thomas had worked there since he was a teenager. He'd simply taken an internship and never left. Thomas was also an avid indexer. He could complete family history charts for several people in a matter of days, when most people needed months or years to do it. His favorite was completing them for famous people and criminals. He had a dark side, which in this case, might work in his favor.

"Hello Tom!" Adam walked in and right up to the desk he'd had most of the time serving in the city. Luckily, Tom was there working. He was at the front desk clicking away on the computer and smiled widely as Adam walked in.

"Adam! Great to see you. How's Julia?" They shook hands as Adam took a seat in front of Tom's desk.

"She and I are expecting." Said Adam, trying not to give much away about what he was doing.

"Congratulations friend! That's wonderful news!" Tom was beaming. He and his wife had three children of their own.

"Yeah, it's pretty exciting. We've been getting into family research ourselves, in order to find the perfect name for our baby. I thought if anyone could help me out, it'd be you." Adam was trying to get the information he needed without raising any alarms. If the mirror people were watching him, he had to be careful about who he trusted.

"Absolutely! Is there a family name from your family you want to see, or maybe Julia's?" Tom started typing on his computer to get into the archives.

"Both would be great! I need 3 boys and 3 girls names." Tom searched. This was just Adam's way of softening Tom up so he could get the information he really needed.

"Ah, here we go." Tom scrolled through a few names while Adam took pen and paper to make his list. "For girls, you both have a lot of Matilda's, Grace, and Annalise. For boys, you have Henry and George as the most used names, but Julia has Harry, Alexander and Charles."

"These are great names. Thank you so much, Tom." Adam stood up but hesitated. Tom took notice.

"Is there anything else I can help you find?" Tom cleared off his home screen and was ready to search again.

"Actually, there is. This is sort of a private matter for a client. He's looking for someone related to the former illusionist, Samuel Grey. He wants to find a current blood relative for a research paper he's doing." Adam added that last bit, as he knew he needed a reason to get a number or an address.

"Ah, ok. So, this is research and history based, I'm assuming." Tom stated. Adam knew that he wouldn't look up living relatives unless it was important.

"Yeah. He was adopted, but this was the only family name he knew. He isn't going to contact anyone, just going to add his birth family to his own family tree." Adam added quickly, trying to make it sound less troublesome.

Tom hopped back on his computer and typed in the information that Adam provided. There were at least six living relatives that were direct descendants of Samuel Grey and his wife Clementine. Tom gave Adam the phone numbers and addresses for each person, just in case his friend changed their mind, and he thanked him, then left.

Adam headed straight back over to James' home to let him know what he found. When Adam got there, he saw James with papers spread out over his bed, scribbling frantically. James grabbed the poker and looked up when Adam entered the room. Seeing who it was, he put the poker down and smiled.

"Adam! I remember some of the stuff from my journal. I'm writing it down just in case we can't get the book back. But we need to make sure these are safe this time." He paused, searching his handiwork for something. "There has to be something here we can use. Maybe another way to defeat them if I can't remember the words to that spell to reverse Grey's mistakes."

Adam nodded. "I have great news for us both too. I have six relatives for Grey. Hopefully, you can remember the incantation, but if not, I hope they know how to fix this mess from their ancestor. Here's hoping we can get the book back either way."

"That's great! Let's hope you can get the book back from Julia tonight. If you can, what I'm doing isn't necessary. But it might be tricky. She did stab me after all. But I hope that one way or another, we can fix this. I can't have another close call like the one I've had already. They are getting stronger. I can hear my reflection whispering to me through the covered mirrors." James's eyes went hazy for a moment. "We need to be prepared." He finished.

"Prepare for them to come through?" Adam asked.

"More than that." James said. "We need to prepare for them to take over and possibly even kill some of us." This was more than just saving them all from the images in the mirror, this was about a war. A war with themselves. They had to fight to keep themselves as they were. Adam liked who he was and didn't want to know what his image reflected of him. According to the research, the mirror images were more than a reflection of themselves, but the opposite of who they were. It was their darker qualities. Who knew what he would find if he came across himself one day.

Adam made sure James had all he needed to work on collecting his thoughts and headed back home to work on getting the book back. This was going to be a challenge. Now that they knew what the mirror Julia was capable of doing to them, he knew that there wasn't much choice in the matter. He had to protect himself from her wrath and get his wife back... if she wasn't already dead. Though Adam had a suspicion that she was still alive for some reason. He couldn't say how he knew; he just did.

Chapter 9

J ames spent most of the night between sleep and writing. It clouded his dreams with the events of the past few months. First, when he was attacked in the bathroom, then when mirror Julia stabbed him and took his book. He was deathly afraid of facing her again though he knew he had no choice. It constantly jerked him awake, and he was writing every detail he could remember, from his book and also the moments he encountered mirror folk before all of this. And his dreams. Who knew if they would come in handy.

He knew that Dr. Swanson was checking in on him. He promised he would. After all, there was a reason he had picked Dr. Adam Swanson in the first place. He had done his own research on him. He KNEW Adam was the one he needed to fix this. Dr. Adam Swanson was adopted as an infant. He did not know this since there was no record of it, but James knew. He was adopted too and he had been in the room, listening to the adults talk about this new boy who was joining them. They dropped a name, Samuel Gray. The family didn't want the name to be associated with anyone in their family line, so they had adopted out the children born to the Gray family directly. Some of the caretakers were not ok with that and kept records, while others didn't. The ones that kept records locked them in filing cabinets and forgot about them while the others just ignored the past and focused on the children's futures.

But not James. He remembered. The paranoia in James had driven him to research everything about everyone in his life. Dr. Swanson was really born as Samuel Grey Jr., the great, great grandson of Samuel Grey. His real name would be connected to his files, but not his adopted name. No one would be able to find him unless they knew he was adopted or were looking for adopted relatives.

James had known all along. He was aware of it all. He was aware of what should have been done and who to search for. James needed Adam to find that out on his own, though. It was the only way for him to build enough confidence in himself to break the curse and close the portal up to the other world. Not that it mattered much, but confidence was key to spells. And anyways, what psychologist would believe his schizophrenic patient if he'd told him he was adopted when he didn't even know that himself? Nope. He had to follow all the breadcrumbs and figure this out on his own. James had the other half to figure out. This spell, or whatever it was, had to be figured out.

James heard the doorbell. It must be Adam. He usually rang before coming in. Partially because he was polite and partially as a warning, so James knew someone was coming. James, out of instinct after what happened, had grabbed the poker from beside his bed. Luckily, James was able to get up and move around better on his own. He walked to the door and Adam was standing there holding a ton of food. Finally, it was time to try eating something real and not just drinking protein shakes.

"Thought you'd like some actual food today since you were on your special throat surgery diet for so long." Adam laughed, and James tried before starting a coughing fit. "Today you can finally start eating soft foods, so I have mac and cheese, mashed potatoes, applesauce, and Jello." Adam was acting extra cheerful and helpful. James knew it was mostly because he didn't want to be at home with mirror Julia, but he appreciated it anyways.

"Thank you. And umm... Julia didn't..." James started, worried that Adam spending all his time at his place would ensue another attack that might include poison this time around.

"No. Mirror Julia didn't make this. I went down to the ready-made food section at the grocery store. Figured that was much safer than trusting a mirror person to cook dinner." Adam said, knowingly.

"Thank you. This really helps." James watched as Adam pulled up one of the dining room chairs and they sat together at the table, munching their food. It was the best thing James had ever eaten. James had pencils and paper all over the counter and it seemed that Adam noticed.

"Been busy with stuff?" Adam asked, looking around the room.

"Yea. I have the pages I'm done with, set in a box under my bed. It's fireproof and locked. I had the box in my closet before but forgot about it till just now. Figured I would put it to good use this time around. At least no one can burn the information I have now." James said.

"That's great! Do you remember the combination?" He asked him, hoping to get this information from him too.

"Yes. It's my birthday. I figured, if anything happened, only the real Adam would know that. It's in my file. Though Julia found me so she might have access to that too." James replied. He knew he was right.

"True. Though I honestly hope not. Maybe change it later. Better safe than sorry this time around. So.... Mirror Julia broke all but three mirrors in my basement at home. Not sure if she knows about those. Been dealing with shards of glass and whispers in every room lately. Hopefully, I won't have much else to deal with until then. I get more worried about the mirrors in the work bathroom and in public anyways. If you're in their alone, you can hear them whisper too." Adam informed James. James wasn't surprised.

"That's not an ideal outcome. This means they are even closer than they were to getting through. That means that it's almost time. Have you found any of the Grey family to close this portal yet?" James asked, hoping he would know his role.

"Yes," Adam replied. "I'm the one to do it. I'm the only one left that's still alive." James tried to look surprised but couldn't.

"I know. I was with you in the orphanage when you were taken in. I heard the adults talk about you and when you became my therapist, I recognized you." James told him.

"Why didn't you tell me?" Adam asked.

"We weren't allowed to talk to you when you first arrived because you were so shut down with depression that we couldn't. But when I was taken in and adopted, we lost contact. Then when I researched and found out who you were, I could only wait for you to realize it too. I didn't want to sound crazy." James told him.

"I see your point. I understand what you mean, now. Thank you for letting me do this one on my own. I appreciate it." Adam told James. They both had their mutual understanding now.

Chapter 10

"So, how'd you find out you were the only left in your family?" James asked Adam as they cleaned up the house. James was still struggling to do things on his own from time to time.

Adam told James how he had gone to visit the people on the list Andrew had given him. He had gone to Millie's house first but had hardly walked in the door when she noticed he looked EXACTLY like her father. She'd known that her parents had given up a child because of a financial situation when they were younger. She had thought of looking for her brother as a teen, but her parents had refused, saying it wasn't worth reopening the pain the adoption had caused the family. She explained why he was adopted and why he had been given away, but she hadn't. They wanted a girl and someone who didn't look like they belonged to one of the Gray's.

Millie had shown him photos of when he was a baby. There were only a few her mom had kept in an album, hidden amongst her things when she'd passed. Clearly, their father hadn't known about it. He was adamant about secrets staying secret and everything going away. Their mother, and Millie, however, took the opposite view. They wanted to keep his memory alive and one day find him again. But it was nearly impossible.

"She told me my mom wanted to find me and had hired a private investigator, but she passed on before they got started." Adam told James.

"How fortuitous. So, you know for a fact now that you are Samuel Grey's grandson?" James asked cautiously, making sure Adam was certain about it.

"I do. Which means that the second you remember those words, I can go to a room of mirrors and fix things." Adam replied.

"A room of mirrors? Mirror me, said nothing about that." James told him.

"I bet. Apparently, Millie said this has happened before and her family had a notebook too. The mirror people tried to gain her trust once before. They only gave her enough information to gain her trust. Then they tried to take her. I have her notes here." Adam pulled out a spiral-bound notebook.

"Does she have the incantation in there?" James asked.

"No. She got the location of where we need to be to close the gate. You got the incantation. Apparently, you only get a bit of information at a time. Either way, we can combine the two. But now there's a third piece of information needed." Adam added.

"What's that?" James asked.

"The location of the room of mirrors. But I'm pretty sure I have an idea." Adam told him, trying to find a map in the junk drawer of James's kitchen.

"Where do you think it is?" James watched Adam rummage through his things like he lived there.

"The old theatre. Grey used the old theatre for his performance, where he opened the portal the first time." Adam replied.

"That makes sense. Go to the source!" James should have thought about that before. If it's where the portal was opened, then it should be the place they need to go to close it up.

"Yea, but is it the right place? It's now being used for community theater and I'm pretty sure it's been renovated at some point in time. So, what if the room isn't there? Then what would we do?" Adam was really contemplating this. He wanted his wife back but felt like maybe they would fail. Would they save his wife? It had been so long since he'd seen her, and she was going to have a baby soon. What would happen if she had the baby before he could save her? James could sense Adam's distress.

"It's going to be ok. We will get Julia and your baby back." He told him, putting a hand on his shoulder.

"Thank you, James. I'm sure we will. But we really need to get everything together now and then get ready to go. I'm pretty sure Mirror Julia is getting suspicious of what we are doing right now. She always seems to be lurking and waiting for me to give something away. I haven't kept any of our information at the house, though. I really hope she doesn't find out any more stuff. I have a feeling that they are going to try to stop us once we start."

"I think you're right. Actually, I know you are. I can't be sure, but I think it was Mirror me that convinced my mirror self to attack me the first time. He wasn't alone when I had been grabbed and he hasn't tried since. Who else would it have been if it wasn't her?" James looked worried.

"If that's true, then we really need to hurry up. I can't waste any more time and neither can you. Do you think you'll be able to remember everything by tomorrow?" Adam asked him, hopeful that he would remember the words to that spell.

"I sure hope so. I only have two words left on the incantation. Once I have them, we should be good to go. Though I still can't recall them to save my life, which is exactly what I need them for." James laughed. Adam knew he was making light of everything to keep himself calm. They both were.

"Great. I will let you rest now and see you in the morning." Adam told him. Adam left James and hoped he'd remember the words to the spell by morning. They needed it desperately and fast.

Chapter 11

When Adam arrived home, the mirror Julia was already in bed asleep. She rarely bothered him while he was there anymore, especially now that she had the book. He knew that in order to release Julia he was going to need a mirror from their house. It didn't need to be the one Julia was caught in, though that'd be ideal, it just had to be there when she was trapped. That was the key. That was the only exception to the rule of using the original mirror.

Most of the mirrors had been destroyed when mirror Julia got out, but Adam knew that there had to be at least one or two left. He opened the door to head into the basement. They had extra home decor down here, tools Adam rarely used, and a holiday hodge podge of crap that got replaced yearly, the usual. He dug around in the mess as quietly as he could, promising to himself that if they ever made it out of this crazy situation, he was going to organize the basement better, maybe even finish it up and add a specific storage room where he can hide things they might need, just in case something weird happened again.

Adam moved boxes and bins full of random, musty smelling décor before finding what he needed. Between the water heater and the fuse box, there were a few boxes with paintings and mirrors in them. That's what he wanted. Luckily, Julia kept items that she meant to give away or sell at yard sales down there too. The first box he'd opened contained a medium-sized, beveled mirror with gold trim. It had been from Julia's gold loving phase before she'd decided silver was better for decorating their home. After concealing it with canvas, he put it in a different box. He had to sneak this out. He would put it in the trunk and get it to his office until he and James could figure out what to do next. Adam stood up, lifted the box, before hearing footsteps. He turned around just in time to see the mirror Julia descend the stairs.

"Going somewhere, honey?" She had a very sinister tone to her voice. How much had she seen and how long had she been there? Adam had to lie.

"I needed a new piece for my office. I knew you had some down here. I thought it'd be the best place to look for art. I thought that this one would be great." He lifted the mirror wrapped in canvas. It looked like art from afar and he hoped that it would convince her.

"I see that. Well, then I guess I'd better leave you to it." She turned and walked up the steps. When she reached the door, Adam heard her slam it and the lock click. CRAP! He was now locked in. Clearly, she hadn't been convinced at all. Frantically, he began searching for a way out. There was a small, locked, window he wouldn't fit out of even if he tried. He kept moving boxes and digging around, looking for something, anything. There had to be something in his old toolbox to pick a lock or smash the window so he could call for help. And what would happen once he got out?

He found a door shaped piece of drywall tucked behind a row of boxes and furniture. It was a long shot. Adam grabbed a sledgehammer and started swinging. Maybe he could smash his way out? Would this lead to the house next door or at least somewhere he could leave? After he hit the wall a few times, he felt a rush of cool air. It smelled of dirt and mold, but that only made him swing harder at it. Even if it was just dirt on the other side, he could try to dig his way out.

He broke through enough to see a tunnel leading out. Adam didn't expect that. He wasn't sure if it was going to be a dead end or not but there was only one way for him to find out. When the hole was big enough to fit him, and the mirror, though, he grabbed what he needed and stepped through. The tunnel was made of dirt, with lots of wooden supports, the kind you'd see in a mine shaft. Was this used as a mine shaft before or was it just a part of the house the previous owners hadn't bothered to finish building? Either way, it was going to save him today.

Walking further down, he noticed that there was something reflective lined up against the walls. Hundreds of mirrors, all shapes, and sizes, somehow collected together in this tunnel, that seemed to extend for several miles. Why were all these mirrors here? What were they for? Adam could hear lots of whispering in the mirrors and even though the tunnel was dark, and he had no light, the mirrors themselves gave off their own light. He noticed there were shadows moving in them, talking to each other. Plotting and planning. He had to keep quiet and not draw attention to himself, lest they should try and get him without a way to escape.

The tunnel continued on for what felt like forever. He felt as if he'd walked all the way into town now at the very least. Eventually, he spotted a ladder that led up to a hatch. He set the mirror down so he could climb up and check the door. The hook under it was rusty, but not too much trouble to unhook. He flipped the top up with a loud creaking and a thud and opened it. Adam climbed down to grab the mirror and shoved it up first before climbing up after it into what looked like an old theatre. This was where the room of mirrors should be. He wasn't sure how he knew it, he just did.

Adam looked around. He was standing backstage, and boxes of old costumes and dusty curtains surrounded him as he set the mirror down and took a breath of freedom. Adam saw a door leading out to the corridor of dressing rooms, with another door leading outside. He knew he needed to look around more but didn't want to do anything alone right now. He decided to call James instead.

"You need to get to the old theater now!" Adam said hurriedly into the phone when James picked up.

"I would, but your wife is standing outside my front door." James' voice was nothing but a whisper. Adams heart sank.

"Hold on then. I'll be right there." Adam rushed out of the theater, ready to rescue James.

Chapter 12

The real Julia paced back and forth in the foggy mirror world. She'd been there for months. She knew it was months because she and the baby were still growing. The fog gave her nourishment, though she didn't know how. She was worried that it would hurt the baby at first, but she was thirsty, and tried to catch the water droplets in her mouth. Once she had, she no longer felt hungry, thirsty, tired, or sick. But she always felt scared, and a bit bored. Other than walking around listening to the other mirror people talk to each other, and of course trying to watch others from their mirrors, she had nothing else to do. Just because nourishment was no longer a concern, didn't mean delivering her baby wasn't. Maybe she could find a doctor in the mirror world and get help? She wasn't sure, but she really wanted to try. Could she even deliver in this world? What would happen to her and the baby?

She really hoped that Adam found a way to get her out. She missed him and being with him in their home. Mirror Julia had been whispering to her for months, but she had no idea how to tell Adam about it. She had even made several attempts to grab her while Adam was at work. One day, the real Julia went to the mirror, wanting to see her baby bump, and the mirror Julia had pulled her in. They had swapped places. What would happen if mirror Julia gave birth in the real world? Would there be a twin for her baby? Would that twin be ready to take her baby's place? Did Adam even know that mirror Julia wasn't her? So many questions with not enough answers.

She'd been listening to the other shadows and mirror people while she tried to find a way to escape. Several other real versions of people had been pulled in, so she wasn't all alone, but that only made her more nervous. They were all scared and confused.

Some of them had been there for years and that made Julia lose some of her hope of ever being freed. Julia tried to help everyone stay as calm as possible. She was trying to be the person that she wished she had when she was taken. It helped for a while, but now anxiety was rising since the mirror people were gearing up to take over everything. What would happen if they did? Would everyone in the world end up in the mirror world?

She listened to the rumors going around about the real world too. At one point, she heard about her mirror self a few times, mostly about her mirror self who had stabbed a man named James in the neck and was now guarding his front door. The real Julia knew that mirror Julia was going to do something bad, and she hoped that James was ok. She hoped that Adam was safe too. She wondered if he would know to go to the old theatre to break the curse on her. Julia heard some of the mirror people talk about that. She kept seeing her husband's shadow on the other side and following him around as much as she could. She could hear him talk about things and this made her glad to know he was at least trying to save her.

One thing she heard was that Samuel Gray was her husband's relative. The man that created this problem in the first place. She knew he'd figure things out and fix what his ancestor had broken. He had to. He was the only one who could. She didn't know anyone else that could since her mirror version had the book James wrote about them. And yes, she knew about that too. She knew Adam was in the basement and saw him through the mirrors. She could only whisper to him though and it didn't seem like he could hear or make out what she was saying when she tried to lead him to the mirrors they had stored down there. She knew he had to hear the whispering in the tunnel under their house, though. She had found those mirrors from the other side on day one. She wanted to help him as much as she could but didn't know how. Maybe there was a way she hadn't discovered yet.

Julia felt along the edge of the mirror world. It was like a map of the real world, but with only reflective surfaces showing through the fog. Puddles of water, car hoods, mirrors, and other reflective surfaces would let her, and the other mirror people see out and others see in. The world was all gray, black, and white. Only those in the real world would ever see color. Julia missed color. Julia looked for a way to talk to her husband again. She also needed to find her mirror self. She had to find a way to stop her from hurting any more people.

Chapter 13

Adam arrived at James's house and Adam could hear James crying out for help in the basement. Adam, not thinking about what he'd just escaped, ran towards him, unlocked the door, and was shoved down the steps by mirror Julia. She had now locked them both in the basement. There was no window and no way to get out. They only had a limited amount of time to get out of there and get to the theater. They needed to find the room of mirrors that Samuel Gray used to open the portal. The real Julia would have her baby soon and there was no way she could do it safely in the mirror world.

"How can we get out of here?" Adam asked James. They were both looking around but Adam wasn't sure they would find a second tunnel leading out unless they were really lucky.

"Well, there might be a tunnel down here somewhere. They built the whole town on top of the old town, so most houses have tunnels and doors in them. I'm not sure if I have one here or not." Adam couldn't believe their luck. James started shifting boxes and other items away from the walls and Adam helped him.

"Yea, that's how I found the way to the theater in my house. I took a mirror from my basement there, after mirror Julia locked me in. Hopefully, you have enough information to help me get the real Julia out of there and put this one back. I don't like her very much." Adam felt a bit defeated but he was trying to lighten the mood a bit so his patient would feel less panicked. It was incidents like this that made his job as a therapist necessary.

"I think so. I had a dream, and I wasn't sure if the words I thought of were right but used them. I think they're right. They sound right to me anyways. Here's hoping all that subconscious stuff you talk about really works." Adam was elated to hear the news and didn't mind the poke at his therapy techniques.

"That's the best news I've heard all day!" They moved things around faster and after about twenty more minutes of shuffling things around, James came across a seam in the wall.

"Adam, come check this out! I think I found it!" Adam rushed over as James dug around in a rusty toolbox looking for a flathead screwdriver. James traced along the seam in the wall as Adam started peeling the paper and plaster away. Sure enough, there was a door with a large, rusty knob. Adam attempted to turn it, but it was locked.

"Dang it! We need to unlock it!" Adam and James looked around on the shelves, in containers, and in the surrounding boxes, looking for any type of old-fashioned, rusty key. On the top shelf of a wooden bookcase, Adam noticed a large mason jar full of keys. He grabbed a stepladder, climbed up, and grabbed it.

"I'm checking this jar. We have to at least find something that will work!" Adam dumped the jar of keys on the ground and started sorting through them. He tried to find one that matched the rusty doorknob. Adam put the keys that he knew wouldn't work back into the jar. In the end, he had about twenty keys to try in the lock.

He started handing keys to James to try in the lock. Each key that didn't work was put back in the jar. "There has to be at least one that fits this old lock!" James complained after the fifth key.

"Keep going. We will find it!" Adam replied encouragingly. After the fifteenth, they found it.

"Got it!" James yelled. "Let's get going. We can find a way out for sure." Adam followed James down a long, dark hallway similar to the one from his basement.

"These tunnels follow our city outline. Depending on where you want to go, you can find anything. We have to get to the old theater. That's where I can save everyone." Adam stated, urging James to make a left, and they headed towards the theater.

Adam noticed one thing weird about the tunnels. They all seemed to branch out into smaller tunnels that lead to the clearing under the theater. That also meant all the roads in town led to the theater too. Everything started looking familiar again, and Adam showed James where to get in. They climbed through the trapdoor and entered the stage. Adam showed James where the hall of doors was. He wasn't sure how he knew where everything was, but it felt like an intuition now. They each took a side and started looking for the room of mirrors, hoping to find it before mirror Julia did.

Chapter 14

Mirror Julia was very familiar with the tunnels under the city too. She knew exactly where Adam and James were going. She knew a faster way to get there. Mirror Julia drove Adam's car over to the graveyard and went into an old mausoleum. At the back, there was a broken horse statue. She 'fixed' the leg, so it aligned with the rest of the leg, and a small door opened at the base. She slipped inside and ran to the center of the tunnels, which was the center of town normally. She hid in the shadows until James and Adam ran past her. Then she followed closely behind them. They climbed up the hatch but didn't shut it behind them. She followed them up to the stage and then to the hallway, where all the hall of doors were, and all the doors led to different rooms. Mirror Julia knew they were looking for the mirror room. She went back to the stage and hid behind the curtains. She saw a small glint of something shiny behind one of the black curtains and moved to investigate it. She saw a mirror. She wasn't sure where it'd come from, but she took it anyways. She followed closely behind, waiting until they found the room of mirrors.

"Here it is!" James called out. Adam raced over to him but froze when he saw mirror Julia holding the mirror from his house, standing at the end of the hallway between the two men.

"James. She's here!" Adam called out, heart sinking as he saw her holding the mirror from his house. James raced out of the room as the mirror Julia walked closer to James, her eyes not leaving Adam for a second.

"Let's go inside the room, shall we?" She gestured to the door James had walked out of.

"What do you want from us? We just want things to go back the way they are supposed to be!" James said. Mirror Julia sneered.

"The way they're supposed to be? You guys don't get it, do you?" Mirror Julia took a few steps closer. "This isn't the world you think it is."

"What do you mean?" Adam asked, stepping closer to her, hoping for a way to get the mirror away from her.

"When Samuel Gray opened the portal, he didn't just open the portal. He did something worse. He trapped REAL people inside the mirror world. It's not just us in there. It's all of us out here and in there and all over the place. You think your parents gave you up for adoption because they wanted to cut off the Gray line, and in a sense they did. But it was more than that. They were mirror people. You're one of us."

"What? How?" Adam felt numb and James looked shocked. How was this even possible?

"Yes. Some of our ancestors are really mirror people and they are living normally out here. Others are just fine and living amongst the mirror folks. It's not just the mirror people that want out. It's normal people that were trapped there, those born in the mirror realm, that want out too. Everyone wants out. That's why it's so hard. Some of us mirror folk want to replace the regular beings, while others want us to live together, and a spare few that want the mirror world to stay the same and the regular world to be what it is. Obviously, I don't agree. I would rather have freedom. The mirror world is full of fog and shadows and this world has color and more to it than the whispering of what we could be. There is no one that I know that would want to live there on purpose. Would you?" Mirror Julia looked at them.

Why couldn't everyone just stay where they were supposed to? Adam could see her manipulation from a mile away. She was trying to get him to feel sorry for them, but it wasn't going to work.

"That means that Julia, the real Julia, is stuck there in the fog and shadow. But what would happen if everyone was living together?" Adam asked.

"Everyone would have a twin and so on. The more real copies of you there are, the more you'll have with the mirror version of yourselves. That would make the world overpopulated and confusing. Not to mention that not all mirror people are nice. Could you imagine having two of the same murderers around? That would be fun now, wouldn't it?"

"You should know." James snapped at her, his scar from her attack showing bright red on his neck. Mirror Julia gave him a half smile.

"Why can't people come and go from both worlds as they please? Have mirror people live in the mirror world then visit us here in the real world?" Adam asked.

"That would work. At least until it didn't. Once mirror people see what you have here that we don't have there, they won't want to leave. There's also the same possibility of trapping each other in mirrors and keeping actual spirits there. Mirrors are used to trap spirits, you know. That's why Victorian people used to cove the mirrors up when people died. They didn't want their spirits to be stuck at home. There are other things that connect to the mirror world. Many of them are monsters. You don't want those to find you either. We have our own enemies. Mostly, they leave people alone in our world. But if they get out, your world will no longer exist. Ever hear of haunted places full of demons? They have already leaked out among you guys. Imagine a world full of them, or worse. Bloody Mary isn't just a game, it's an invitation to those monsters to get out. And don't get me started with a spirit board. That is like a phone call to the mirror world. Spirits and mirror people hear that call. Yes, they do both exist." She finished as Adam and James stood openmouthed in shock.

"Look, I can chat with you all day about the secrets of our world, but right now, I want to let my fellow mirror folks out and take charge. So why don't you guys stand in that corner and wait for your turn to go to the other side," she said, pointing to a large mirror with a tight spot beside it, "and I will summon up some folks." She had a bag that neither of the guys had noticed before, and she had pulled out a spirit board and set it next to the mirror that Adam had brought from home.

"What are you doing?" Adam shouted at her. She had just begun to position mirrors in the room they were in, in such a way that they formed a circle. Adam's mirror being placed in the center.

"I found this bonus mirror backstage. I will be breaking it so the real me will have a much harder time getting back to you. Good luck trying to decode what you have to do now, fellas." And she got to work.

Chapter 15

Adam looked at James. "What now? Do you know what I have to do to stop this from happening?" James held a finger up to his lips and pointed to a mirror that was covered up with a black cloth.

"You have to uncover that mirror. That was the original mirror used in Gray's portal mishap. If you open that, stare into it and say the spell, all the mirror people will disappear, then the regular people will go back. It should be fairly simple, but getting to the mirror to uncover it, and say the words without her hearing them will be tricky." James looked around to create a distraction. "We have to catch her off guard. Maybe split up."

"I know. What if I offer to break the mirror? I will distract her, and you can uncover the mirror while I save the mirror Julia is in. I won't break it; I will read the words too. I have them memorized. If we do that, then maybe we can stop her and this whole thing from happening."

"Ok. Let's do it now." Adam told him. He rushed over to the mirror with the black cloth on it and pulled fabric off. Adam looked at the words on the paper that James gave him. Revertere in speculum in perpetuum. Latin. Of course. James was slowly approaching the mirror while mirror Julia was distracted by Adam.

"Stop it!" She howled. Adam stopped, not sure what to do as she took a few steps towards him.

James had almost made it to the mirror when mirror Julia looked back at him too now, realizing what they were doing. "I know what you're doing, and I don't think that it is wise of you to betray me right now. I know everything about you. You are one of the Born. Half mirror person and half human. That' why your mirror self was able and willing to talk to you so freely. You do not know what will happen to you if Adam sends everyone back." She sang the last bit, adding to the already creepy vibe in the room.

"I don't care what happens to me. I just want the rest of you gone! Mirror people killed my father for not being a mirror person. My mother has already died. There is nothing left for me, but my adopted family and you took them, too. I want mirror people gone. This isn't where you belong!" James rushed forward just as the mirror Julia leapt towards him. He grabbed the black cloth off the mirror and shouted at Adam, "NOW!"

Adam looked at the paper as mirror Julia turned towards him to attack, then said, "I will break Julia's mirror. Mirror Julia is right. She deserves to be here." Mirror Julia smiled. James looked shocked before realizing what Adam was doing and playing along.

"See? I knew you'd see it my way. Just wait till you meet your mirror self. He is a great guy. Go ahead and break your wife's mirror. Keep her trapped." Adam walked forward and picked it up. He had to do this right so he could save her. Adam went back to the corner and aimed her mirror towards the mirror Julia. He held the slip of paper behind the mirror as he raised it up.

"Revertere in speculum in perpetuum!" He replied loudly. There was a loud scream but not from the mirror Julia. This sound came from James, as he was literally being torn in half. Mirror Julia stared at him.

"See? Now you'll be stuck in the mirror world with me forever!" She said as she was being slowly sucked into the mirror. Regular Julia was materializing in her place. "At least you have one less patient now." Mirror Julia mocked him before screaming and following James into the mirror.

Both James and mirror Julia were gone, and the real Julia was back. "Adam! I missed you so much! I thought I wouldn't get out before the baby came!" They embraced.

"I didn't think you would either, to be honest, but I'm glad you're home now." He said, examining her and putting his hand on her belly, large with child.

Julia grabbed at her stomach. "The baby is on its way now. We need to go. The stress of that transition was difficult." She said, bending over slowly and clutching at her side. Adam saw his car in the parking lot and realized the mirror version had taken it. Luckily for him, she left the keys in the car and they headed to the hospital. There, Julia delivered a boy.

"That's a surprise. I am glad, though." Adam said as he held his son. "Could we name him James? James Samuel?" Adam asked her, wanting to remember his former patient but also not forgetting the ancestor who accidentally created this mess in the first place.

"I think that would suit him. And Adam, I am glad that James helped you out. I really wish I had listened to you and told you what was going on from the beginning." Julia told him kissing his cheek then their baby's head.

"It's ok. I'm just glad we made it out alive, even if James didn't." Adam was glad to have his family back home with him.

"Same here. We should really get rid of all the mirrors at home, though. I don't think I want that to happen again." Julia added.

"Well... maybe we can keep one. Just in case I can talk to the other James if he's on the other side." Adam said, realizing that he was also part mirror person. Though if James was too, then why did he go back in the mirror and Adam didn't? This would be research for another day.

Don't miss out!

Visit the website below and you can sign up to receive emails whenever Abby Woodland publishes a new book. There's no charge and no obligation.

https://books2read.com/r/B-A-JGXZ-OUOWC

Connecting independent readers to independent writers.

Did you love *In the Mirror*? Then you should read *Secrets in the Woods*[1] by Abby Woodland!

2

Ella and her family moved to a small town with dark secrets. The woods holds something inside of it that has the residents scared and Ella wants to find out what it is. Her only source of information comes from the antique shop in town where an old woman gives her a doll that's connected to the secrets. When the doll behaves strangely, Ella must go back and talk to the shop keepers grandaughter, who in turn, helps her find the spell to break through the curse and bring peace back to their small town, but at a price.

1. https://books2read.com/u/bp1q19

2. https://books2read.com/u/bp1q19

Read more at www.abbywoodland.com.

Also by Abby Woodland

The Raze
The Dragon Keeper
Birchwood
The Fairwing School for Troubled Girls
While She Sleeps
Secrets in the Woods
In the Mirror

Watch for more at www.abbywoodland.com.

About the Author

Abby Woodland lives in Arizona with her daughter and large extended family. She is a musician, prepper, and complete book nerd. If she's not writing, she's editing, playing guitar, going on walks, or advocating for mental health and those with special needs.

Read more at www.abbywoodland.com.

Milton Keynes UK
Ingram Content Group UK Ltd.
UKHW012014290224
438689UK00001B/27